May 2014

For Samuel –

Marcia H. Carter

A hundred years from now it will not matter
What my bank account was,
The sort of house I lived in
Or the kind of car I drove —
But the world may be different
Because I was important in the life of a child.

Ora's Farm

Marcia H. Carter

Illustrated by J. B. Wonderling

Black Sands Enterprises
Canton, Georgia

Printed in the United States of America

Published by:
Black Sands Enterprises
P.O. Box 4382
Canton, Georgia 30114-0017
(770) 281-3101
http://www.blacksands.com

Interior Design & Typesetting:
Desktop Miracles, Inc., Stowe, Vermont

Library of Congress Cataloging-in-Publication Data

Carter, Marcia H.
    Ora's farm / Marcia H. Carter.
    p.   cm.
    ISBN 0-9671781-1-8
                                          2001117131
                                             CIP

ACKNOWLEDGEMENTS

*My editors, Wanda Bernhardt
and Robert Wilson.*

My artist, Jim Wonderling.

*Special thanks to Sheree and
Leah for leading me to Ora.*

Dedicated to Farmer Ora Coleman,
who is truly a gift from God.

To Stephen Beam, my precious son.

For Jessica Walden, wherever you are.

For Kristin & Nathan Carter, the children who grew
inside my heart, instead of just beneath it.

For Lauren & Brit, the apples of my eye.

And for Stephanie and Ron, my lighthouse
and my strength, as always.

One

ROSWELL, GEORGIA

"Hey, Jessica, want to go with me to Ora's?" Stephen asked.

"No, I'm having a tea party," Jessica answered and Stephen realized her dolls and her koala bear, Sydney, were in a circle around a make believe table.

"Suit yourself," he said as he went on his way.

Jessica was two different people inside one body, Stephen decided. Sometimes she played with dolls and was prissy, other times she would put on blue jeans and become the best tomboy in the world. She would ride her bike really fast and then slam on the brakes and slide. She even blew a tire once. Another redeeming quality was some of the things she said. *Gag me with a maggot* was pretty cool, coming from a girl, Stephen thought.

Jessica had the face of an angel, but not the attitude. Her hair was long and her face was slender, she had a cute little dimple and her blue eyes laughed when she did.

She lived in a fancy three story cluster home just down the street from Stephen. He lived in a house that had been there before the street got so fancy. He had to pass her house to get to Ora's and he always asked if she wanted to go. Sometimes she did, sometimes she didn't.

As Stephen left his street and walked down the older main road, he could see that the gate to Ora's was open. Ora had no phone. Everyone knew they were more than welcome if the gate was open, they knew they should go home if it was closed. It was that simple.

Jessica's mom was raised on a farm and was happy to be gone from it, living in her fancy cluster home. Stephen wasn't sure what kind of farm she had lived on, but he figured it probably wasn't like

Ora's farm. Ora's farm was the kind of place one would expect a spider like Charlotte to take residence and spin a miraculous web or something.

"Hey—wait up!" Jessica called and Stephen turned to see her running behind him. "Changed my mind," she said and Stephen smiled as he waited for her.

Stephen had sandy blonde hair and a cowlick and Jessica thought he was really cute, but she never planned to tell him.

"Where is Kristin?" Stephen asked her.

"She's your next door neighbor, don't *you* know?"

He shook his head. "She's been gone a long time."

"A whole week," Jessica said, as puzzled as he was.

Ora recognized Jessica and Stephen immediately as they walked down the long dirt driveway. He waved and called out *hello* to them in his friendly, *I'm so really glad to see you* way. "Kristin not with you?" he asked the two of them as they got closer.

"No, she's not home," Stephen said. "Her whole family has been gone all week. I don't know where."

Ora looked sad, but Stephen didn't know why. Ora was putting a blanket over his gardenias because he had heard it might frost. It felt too warm to put a

blanket on anything to Stephen, but he was only seven. Kristin and Jessica were seven, too, and Stephen had known them for two years. That's how long it had been since Stephen's mom and dad had gotten a divorce and he and his mom had moved into the neighborhood.

Jessica went to see the rabbits and Stephen grabbed an edge of the blanket to try and help Ora cover the gardenias, but the gardenia bush was taller than he was.

"I'm sure Kristin will be back soon," Ora said kindly and Stephen nodded.

Stephen and Kristin's houses had separate driveways, but a common slab of cement joined them together at one point. Someone had made the driveway that way so a car could be turned around easily, but to Kristin and Stephen, it was their mutual place. They rode their bikes through the turn around spot and they sat on it at night and talked. Stephen's basketball goal stood right at the edge of the concrete and he and Kristin played basketball in the mutual spot also. He had taught her to dribble and shoot and she had rapidly become the best girl basketball player in the neighborhood. She could even outshoot most of the boys.

Kristin lived with her mom and dad and her brother, Nathan. Jessica lived with her mom and her stepfather. Stephen lived with just his mom. He thought the other kids were lucky to have a dad or a stepdad around their house, but Jessica told him that she thought *he* was lucky.

She said that she could see his house from her bedroom on the third floor and she told him that sometimes she watched him and his mom out in the yard. Sometimes his mom was working on her flowers and talking and laughing with him as she worked and sometimes she would throw him a baseball over and over so he could practice hitting it.

Stephen had asked Jessica if she had noticed that his mom couldn't pitch very well and that her shoulder always started to hurt after so many throws. Jessica said she hadn't noticed that, she just saw them having a good time. She said that sometimes even after it was dark and she had been sent upstairs to her bedroom to go to sleep, she would see them on the front porch, still talking.

Stephen told her that his dad could pitch for nine innings and not even be tired. His dad was the coach of his little league team. He knew that his dad loved him and he knew that his mom loved him, but he still wished they all lived together. Then his dad could pitch to him more and he would get better and better and maybe even be a famous baseball player for the Atlanta Braves someday.

"What's troubling you?" Ora asked the little one who was so lost in thought he hadn't even run up to see the goats yet.

Stephen told Ora that he might not be able to play for the Atlanta Braves because he didn't have his dad at home to help him practice a lot.

Ora's blue eyes widened, then his head moved downward with a quick little jerk without the rest of his body moving, as he did a lot.

"Life isn't perfect, you know. This old world could be a lot better than it is if folks went by some of God's rules and stuff, but they don't and it's not and we have to live with it."

"What rules?" Stephen asked as Ora continued to cover the gardenias.

"Take the golden rule, for instance. If everyone treated their neighbor as they would like to be treated, wouldn't this be a wonderful place?"

Stephen wasn't sure what that had to do with his parents' divorce, but he nodded. He and Kristin and Jessica always treated each other that way and it worked pretty well. Besides, Stephen took Ora's word as the gospel truth. Ora's track record spoke for itself. He was never wrong, as far as Stephen knew.

"If it's meant for you to be a player for the Braves, you will be, if it's not, you won't," Ora said kindly. "No use worrying too much about it and don't ever make baseball your God."

"Is that a baby crying?" Stephen asked suddenly.

"Why, it sure is!" Ora said with all the enthusiasm of a new mother, proud to show off her young. "Come on!" he said as he hurriedly put the last blanket on the bush. He was so excited, he was having a hard time moving as fast as he wanted to move.

"I thought it was a real baby," Stephen laughed as Ora picked up a little black billy goat.

"Well, it is," Ora said seriously. "It's only three days old."

Stephen would have laughed, but Ora was serious. He loved his animals as if they were his children.

"There's new rabbits, too. Want to hold one?"

"I want to hold the billy goat."

"Be my guest, but watch out for the mama goat," Ora said, handing him the little bundle.

Stephen walked around, holding the little goat, its bleating causing the mama to follow Stephen, but that was all. The animals trusted Ora to the extent of trusting his friends. If Stephen was a friend of Ora's, he was a friend of theirs. But the mama goat still wished Stephen would put the kid down. Kind of.

Stephen followed Ora down the hill toward the rabbits, eggs of all kinds in every nook and cranny. "What kind of egg is that?" Stephen asked, nodding

toward a cluster of large eggs, his arms full of bleating billy goat.

"Banny eggs," Ora answered.

Stephen's blue eyes widened. "But they're as big as the banny!"

Ora laughed. "I'm a kidding. They're goose eggs."

The geese waddled toward their eggs rapidly, lest their goslings hatch suddenly and meet with the same fate as the young billy goat. Stephen stopped and looked at the fancy chickens.

"You still like those chickens with the feather shoes, huh?" Ora asked.

Stephen nodded as he stood by the feather legged Cochins. The feathers on their legs were so thick and fluffy they extended over their feet, looking like fancy feathery shoes.

"Listen at that sound. Isn't it the most peaceful sound?" Ora asked and even the billy goat was reverently silent.

"What is it?" Stephen asked of the low cooing.

Ora opened the door of a large wooden structure. "Doves," he said quietly and Stephen looked in at the gray and white birds. Ora picked one up and held it gently to him. "They're the sweetest little birds. They make a better pet than a parakeet. Parakeets are annoyingly loud."

The little billy goat chose that time to also become loud, his bleating sounding like a baby in distress and the doves became upset. The ruckus inside their wooden home sounded like the shuffling of a hundred birds instead of twenty.

Ora began to talk to the doves in an ever so soothing voice and Stephen watched in amazement as they all calmed down. Then Ora walked toward Stephen with the dove in his hand and calmed the little billy goat. Stephen was glad because even though the little goat was only three days old, his hoofs were hard pushing against him. Ora then put the dove on his shoulder and walked onward toward the rabbits.

"Why doesn't the dove fly away? Are his wings fixed so he can't fly?" Stephen asked.

"No, I'd never clip their wings. He just doesn't want to go anywhere."

Ora's was the best place in the world for any animal to be and Stephen was glad they all realized it.

"What happened to the turkey?" Jessica asked, joining them. She pointed at a very fat turkey waddling across the yard with quite a few tail feathers missing.

"A fox. He had a very close encounter with a fox," Ora said, turning around to face Jessica. "I've never seen anything like it," he said, motioning with his hands as he always did. "The fox ate eggs all over the place, got a hold of the turkey by the tail feathers, grabbed one of the chickens by the leg and pulled his leg right off. But the chicken stood firm. It didn't surrender and it didn't die. It hops, though. Has no choice. Next time, that fox is gonna find himself lined up in the sights of my shotgun. The coward took off when I came flying out the door."

Stephen looked out across the vast farm. He had never thought of it being invaded by a fox or a wolf. He had thought if a fox or a wolf stepped on the ground here, it would be tame and nice like the other animals. But, as Ora said, life wasn't perfect.

Ora opened the wooden door to a rabbit house he had constructed and pulled a tiny hairless little rabbit out. "Look at him—it'nt that something?" Ora asked "His eyes aren't even open yet. God—it's so pretty. What about that?" he asked, seemingly in awe, then began talking directly to the little rabbit.

Stephen wondered how Ora could continue to be amazed at a new baby rabbit. "Seems like you always have baby rabbits," he said.

"That's the way it is with rabbits," Ora said matter of factly. "Remember how I told you about the mama rabbit making a nest for the babies?"

"Yes. With some of her hair," Jessica answered.

Ora nodded. "Look at this."

A lot of hair was mixed in with the shavings Ora had placed in the cage. Then Stephen saw the mama rabbit. She was absolutely bald in places. Stephen was so amazed he put the billy goat down. The mama goat sighed relief and the two animals took off, as fast as the little one's legs would go.

Stephen stared at the biggest bald spot, on the mama rabbit's chest. "She's a really good mama, I guess."

"She means to be, but she really didn't have to go to that extreme. It's not even very cold."

"My mama goes to extremes sometimes, too," Stephen said, thinking of how his mom tried to do more than her share to make up for the divorce.

"God, there's nothing like a mama," Ora said. Ora said *God* a lot, but it wasn't like he was using it just as an expression, which Stephen and Jessica would have gotten in trouble for at home. It was as if Ora were addressing God personally. Stephen wouldn't be surprised if he were. God probably talked to Ora all the time, too.

Ora smiled wistfully and Stephen knew he was thinking about his own mama. Ora had once told Stephen he would always miss his mama no matter how many years she had been *gone on*.

Stephen and Jessica had to go home without even playing in the pasture. They never had enough time to do everything they wanted to do when they were at Ora's. Stephen waved to the cows as they left and they laughed at the billy goats that were playing in a rusted truck and car down in the pasture.

"One of these days, that one might drive off with my truck," Ora teased, pointing at a brown billy goat comfortably sitting behind the steering wheel. "I'll have to call the cops on him—bad as I hate it."

Stephen and Jessica laughed as they ran past the elephant garlic down the long dirt driveway. They were still laughing when they got to Jessica's—as a matter of fact, they were laughing so hard they lay down and rolled in the grass of her front yard.

Two

STEPHEN FOUND OUT THAT NIGHT why Kristin had been gone. He found out quite by accident. After his mom made him wipe his feet several times as she always did after he had been over at the farm, she had started dinner. As they ate, he looked out the window at Kristin's dark house. "Are they ever coming home?" he asked.

His mom got the same sad look on her face that Ora had gotten when they had talked about Kristin's absence and Stephen frowned.

"Did Kristin die or something and nobody's telling me?" he demanded.

"Of course not."

His mom scurried him off to the shower and he assumed it was because he had been over at the farm playing with the animals and maybe she thought he didn't smell so good. But, when he came back out to get some soap from the hall closet, he heard her talking seriously to a neighbor downstairs. She was saying that Kristin's mother was really sick and they were at a hospital far away trying to make her well, but it hadn't worked.

—w—

Kristin's family came home the next day and Stephen decided there must be a mistake. Kristin's mom looked fine. Had he dreamed all that or what?

"Let's go to Ora's!" Kristin screamed.

They took off on their bikes and when they saw that the gate was open, they hit hands happily, almost losing their balance. They rode rough on the dirt driveway and found Ora sitting peacefully, watching the cows.

"Can I feed them?" Kristin asked.

"That's what I was waiting for," Ora smiled. "You to show up and feed them."

Kristin was glad her family had come back when they did, since Ora was waiting for her to come and feed the cows.

"Come with me, we'll turn the electricity to the fence off," Ora said to Stephen. Kristin took the top off a huge container and filled her hands with grain, then held both hands out toward the cows. The cows saw her and began to walk up the hill quickly, as cow walking goes, although it still may have appeared slow to others.

Kristin giggled as the cows' big rough tongues grazed over her hands and Stephen appreciated a girl that could do that. "That's Betsy and that's Baby, right?" Kristin asked.

"That's right," Ora nodded and Stephen wondered if Kristin had noticed that every female cow was called Betsy and every calf was called Baby. Every bull was called Bull, although they were in a different part of the pasture, so the kids could walk through this one without worry.

"Are all bulls mean?" Stephen asked.

"Just show offs, I think," Ora answered. "Although, some are just plain mean. We had the meanest bull in the world when I was a kid," he said.

"Meanest in the whole world?" Kristin asked.

"No joke," Ora nodded, his blue eyes serious. "You see, we had 104 acres back then. We had sheep and pigs and horses as well as all these other animals."

Stephen didn't ask why he didn't have horses and sheep and pigs anymore, although he wanted to. He thought it might be because Ora just couldn't keep up with all that anymore, so he definitely wouldn't bring it up.

"There were six of us boys and Mama and Daddy," Ora said. "All six of us boys were scared to death of the bull. No matter where we put the bull, he would get out and get in here with the cows, you see. And we had to go down this path to the creek to take a bath."

"You took a bath in the creek? For real?" Kristin asked.

"For real," Ora repeated, the words sounding strange coming from him. "You see, I went ahead and put some tubs in for the cows out here, 'cause I didn't want them having to walk to the creek to bathe." He pointed at the porcelain bathtubs full of water in the pasture. Stephen knew the bathtubs were really there for drinking water for the cows and he snickered.

"Anyway," Ora continued, "we'd get out of the creek, all nice and clean and be on our way back to the house and here'd come that bull and we'd scatter, screaming. My brothers were grown and they'd climb trees and stuff. I couldn't climb very well, so I just had to run. The funniest thing, though, my mama wasn't afraid of the bull. And the bull knew it. Mama was a little woman—barely five feet tall, but she wasn't afraid of anything, as far as I know."

"What did the bull do when he saw your mama?" Kristin asked.

"Acted nice and polite like he had never been a bully. He would follow her around the pasture, calm as anything. Mama wore long skirts and granny boots—you know the little ankle boots. And she worked hard. She washed clothes in the creek, she fed the animals, she worked a garden, a big garden and she cooked and canned and made jelly."

"Did you help?" Kristin asked.

"You better believe it," he nodded. "We all worked hard. I plowed the fields, I fed the animals, I milked the cows, did whatever I was told because that's just the way it was. My daddy said do it and we did it."

"Did you ever get to play?" Stephen asked.

"Oh, good Lord, yeah, we played as hard as we worked. Oh, God, yeah. We used to swim in the creek all the way to where it runs into the Chatta-hoochee River and then we'd have to walk back. Sometimes we'd have to run back because we'd see the sun going down and my daddy didn't put up with being late for dinner. Then there were more chores."

"More?" Kristin asked.

"Oh, yeah. We had to cut up firewood and all kinds of things. It takes a lot to run a big farm. Do you know what our favorite food was?"

"Steak," Kristin guessed. She was pretty sure it was everybody's favorite, especially guys. It was her brother's very favorite.

"No. You see, we had so much of that," he said, pointing at the cows and Kristin cringed. She really didn't like to think about the fact that steak came from a cow.

"We had all kinds of sausage and pork from the pigs and steak and hamburgers from the cows and we had plenty of chicken and all kinds of vegetables from the garden. What we didn't have was junk food. So—sometimes Daddy would go into town and he

534

234a..44

would come back with hot dogs and potato chips and cokes and candy. Now that was a feast."

Kristin and Stephen laughed, trying to imagine hot dogs as a feast.

"Look at that goat—trying to steal my truck again," Ora said as the goat climbed into the torn driver's seat.

Stephen lapsed into giggles. "Let's go see them," he said to Kristin and Ora bade them go. They climbed through the gate to the pasture, a gate that leaned perilously toward the ground after all these years. Had the animals wanted to escape, they probably could have, but of course, they didn't want to.

"You know," Kristin said, looking at the bathtubs filled with water, "as many times as I've been here, I've never seen a cow in one of those bathtubs. And you'd think they'd need a bath at least once a day—I mean, well, they use the bathroom and then they walk in it and stuff. And flies get on them and —"

She thought Stephen was having an attack of some kind he was gasping and choking and coughing and wheezing so badly. But it all stemmed from the fact that he had lost his breath laughing at her.

"What?" she demanded. "And how exactly do the cows fit in there, anyway? I bet the water sloshes out."

Stephen lay on the ground and rolled. Ora turned to make sure he was all right. He had never heard noises quite like the boy was making, he thought at first, but then he realized he had. It sounded like his own laughter when he was young.

"You're going to roll in cow crap," Kristin said, staring at Stephen as if he had gone mad. "And—I don't care if you do," she added.

Stephen tried and tried to regain his breath to tell her why he was laughing, but he would lose it again in another gale of uncontrolled laughter and just lay back down on the ground.

A cow walked past him at very close range and Kristin hoped it would step on him.

The cow, however, walked past him and Kristin stared as it walked up to the bathtub and began to—drink.

"Oh," she said simply and spun on her heel, heading down the hill toward the goats.

Three

STEPHEN KEPT HIS EYES ON the situation next door and Kristin's mom continued to look fine. He realized that if what he had heard were true, Kristin didn't have a clue. But he chose to believe that there had been a mistake.

Kristin's brother was a teenager and Stephen studied his face to try and gain some insight. But Nathan's face always looked serious, even when he was playing, so he couldn't tell.

Stephen talked to Jessica about it and after a lot of thought and some research on her own, Jessica agreed that there had to be a mistake. She said that

Kristin's mom even made cookies with them when she was over for a visit.

—∞—

"Is Dad picking me up today or what?" Stephen asked his mom.

"I'm not sure. He's out of town and it doesn't look like he's going to make it back until tomorrow. If he doesn't get here, we'll go do something special, OK?"

Stephen fought the tears. He didn't want his mom to see him cry because he knew she tried very hard. So he choked it back and went outside.

Stephen didn't mean to be a world class eaves-dropper, but it seemed that lately he was—and he was overhearing more stuff than he wanted to hear. He heard his mom and dad talking about his dad taking a job in another state, somewhere out west.

"Ask Kristin if she would like to go to a movie with us tonight," his mom said from the door. She had apparently just decided that even if his dad did make it in, she would say *too bad, we have plans*. She didn't like it when his dad did things like this.

"I'd love to," Kristin answered his mom without being directly asked as she rounded the house on her bike. "I'll ask my parents."

Stephen's mom thought Kristin was such a cute little girl. Her freckles and her smile went hand in hand with her personality. She was bubbly.

"They said I can go," she said a few minutes later.

"Cool," Stephen said.

—⚬⚬—

Stephen decided that night that he might want to marry Kristin someday. He liked the way she listened to him and laughed at things he said until her eyes crinkled almost closed. And when they would talk about school and stuff, she would agree with things he said with a serious nod of her head, her light brown hair bouncing in its pony tail as she did.

Stephen woke up in a good mood the next morning for many reasons. His eighth birthday was just around the corner, school was almost out and he still planned to marry Kristin someday.

He went outside and made sure the front door closed loudly, so Kristin would hear it. It worked and she soon joined him, but she didn't look happy.

"What's wrong?" he asked as they sat down on their mutual turn around spot of the driveway.

"My mother is dying," she said flatly.

Stephen felt as if a lightning bolt had hit him. He didn't know what to say.

"She and Daddy just told us and I didn't know what to say and I said something really stupid."

"What did you say?"

"I was sitting there, staring out the window because I didn't want them to see me cry and I saw your house and I said, 'Can I tell Stephen?' That was a stupid thing to say." A tear rolled down her cheek.

"What did they say?'

"They said, yes, I could tell you."

"But—she looks OK," Stephen said, thinking it was probably a more stupid thing to say than what Kristin had said.

"She has cancer. She got it five years ago when I was two. I don't remember it, but she had an operation and she was OK. They thought she was going to be OK forever, but it came back and we went to Washington to a research hospital and she and Daddy have been other places, too, but it can't be fixed this time."

Stephen wanted to scream for help, this was over their heads, he didn't know what to do. But Kristin's dad called her and she went in and Stephen ran, not walked, to Ora's.

—ᘯ—

The first thing he saw was the rabbit who had plucked herself bare for her babies and he began to cry. He remembered Ora's words that there was nothing like a mama. Mamas didn't move out west

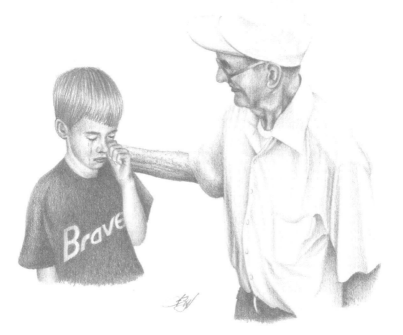

and leave their kids, either. And Kristin was going to lose her mother.

He was wiping tears with the back of his hand when Ora got to him, feed bucket in his hand.

"What's wrong?" Ora asked, concerned.

"Kristin—her mom—"

Ora sighed and put the feed bucket down. "I know," he said kindly. "They tell Kristin today?"

Stephen nodded, his shoulders racked with sobs.

Ora bent down to make himself Stephen's size and though he didn't say a word, the comfort was there.

"Remember when you said you wanted to line that fox up in the sights of your gun and shoot him?" Stephen asked through his sobs.

"Yeah," Ora nodded.

"That's the way I feel right now."

"But who would you shoot?" Ora asked patiently.

"I don't know," Stephen cried. "But it's not fair."

"Come help me feed the cows and we'll talk."

Stephen helped feed the cows and then he filled the bathtubs with water from the hose and freed a billy goat that was stuck in the abandoned truck, Ora talking all the while. Wiping sweat, Ora went inside and returned with two cold green cans of tangy citrus beverage. He and Stephen drank, Ora assuring him that Kristin would survive this cruel blow, that God had a reason for everything.

"Will God tell Kristin's mother the reason when she gets there?"

"I expect so and I believe that she'll look back down from Heaven and know that Kristin and Nathan are fine. God will let her see that."

"He will?"

Ora nodded, his heart full of compassion for the little boy. He reached down and hugged him, then

mapped out the game plan. "Kristin's dad is gonna work double time to help those two kids through this and *your* job is to be an even better friend than you already are and *my* job—well, my gate will be open all the time. I won't even close it at night."

"OK."

"You see that bunny?" Ora asked and Stephen nodded as a brown bunny passed by. "She's the toughest on the farm. The other bunnies respect her. Her mama died when she was a tiny baby. After that, she figured nothing worse could happen to her, so she was ready to face any challenge. She knew that if she had survived losing her mama, she didn't have to be afraid of anything else. She didn't sweat the small stuff, like other bunnies might. The obstacles thrown at you along life's way are a test of character. They make you who you are."

Stephen's mom turned in and he realized he had been gone longer than he thought. He also realized that he hadn't told her where he was going. She wasn't mad, just got out and hugged Ora and they said a few words, probably about Kristin's mother, then Ora gave her baskets of plants and some tomatoes from his garden and walked them to the car.

Four

KRISTIN'S MOM DIED BEFORE she turned eight. Kristin seemed to be in a daze, just doing what people told her to, like a zombie. Stephen's mom told him that the dazed feeling was part of being in shock, your body's way of dealing with something like that.

Kristin and Stephen talked about third grade, but she said that she and her brother and her dad might move and she might not be going to school with him. But how could he be the best friend in the world like Ora told him to if she didn't live next door? And what about all those nights when they sat outside and talked? Who would Kristin talk to now?

—w—

Stephen's dad left for Arizona as soon as baseball season was over and Kristin's dad bought a house across town. She would be moving in a month. Stephen was upset, and he knew Kristin was too, but she still just acted like a zombie.

They sat on the concrete slab turn around spot and didn't say much. Stephen didn't know what to say.

"Do you ever feel like things are moving too fast and you can't keep up?" Kristin asked.

"Yes," Stephen nodded. "Until I go to Ora's."

Kristin smiled. Things definitely didn't move fast with Ora. One time, Ora was using a slider saw to cut some wood and something distracted him, he couldn't remember what. The slider saw was horseshoe shaped and when Ora laid it down, it kind of wrapped around an oak tree. He said he had laughed because it looked as if someone was playing a big game of horseshoes.

Ora had planned to go back and get the saw and continue what he was doing, but other things came up and by the time he tried to move the saw, the tree had grown so much, the saw wouldn't move. He said he knew that if he pulled his tractor up there and gave the slider saw a tug with a rope, it would come from around the tree, but he got busy and the next thing he knew, the tree had grown slap through the slider saw.

It was a strange sight, the slider saw and the wood, the wood having somehow found a way to mold itself around the metal of the slider saw as it grew. Ora just put a swing in the tree and gently pushed the kids in the swing, telling them the story of what had happened as if it had all taken place over the space of a few days instead of many years.

—⟋⟍—

Feeling the need for a place where things never moved fast, they spent a lot of time at Ora's before Kristin moved. She was less the zombie at Ora's than anywhere else and Ora said things that summer that Stephen, Kristin and Jessica would remember forever.

"On summer days like today, I can remember swimming in the creek with my brothers like it was yesterday," Ora smiled. "I told you we used to bathe in the creek, didn't I?"

Stephen nodded.

"Mama had a wash hole down there, too. She'd take her scrub board and all the dirty clothes and she'd wash the better part of a day once a week. Thursday. That was the day." The look on his face was wistful.

"Where do your brothers live now?" Jessica asked.

"I only have one left and he lives in Texas. The other four have *gone on* as my mama and my daddy have. I never call it dying because that's not what it is. They just go on to exist in another place. A better place than here. "

Stephen noticed that Ora had Kristin's undivided attention, but Ora didn't act as if he were talking to anyone in particular.

"And I don't think dying is a horrible, painful thing," he continued matter of factly. "I think when I die, it'll just be like closing my eyes and pretending I'm swimming down the creek in the deep spots like we used to do. But instead of ending up in the river, I'll end up in Heaven with my brothers and my mama and daddy standing there waiting for me. My daddy will probably ask me what took me so long," he smiled fondly. "He always used to ask me that."

Kristin smiled at him through tears.

"And, you know, as much as I enjoy this life here, can you just imagine how much I'm gonna like the next one? It'nt that something? To imagine a place better than here, even?" he asked with a genuine smile and Kristin nodded, smiling also.

Ora looked out across the pasture contentedly and the three kids did the same. After a little while, a turkey waddled by, followed by four baby guineas and Stephen looked at the sight strangely, then looked at Ora.

"The fox got their mama before they were born," Ora answered Stephen's unanswered question. He leaned forward in his chair as he often did to better tell his story. "The mama guinea wouldn't leave the eggs 'cause she knew the fox would get them. So, unfortunately, the fox got her, then I stormed out and the fox took off and there were the eggs. The eggs hatched the next day and the turkey took over from there. What about that? I've never seen anything like it. No joke," Ora said with an emphatic nod of his head.

Stephen smiled, sure that things like this could only happen at a place like Ora's, but then he thought of the mother guinea protecting her babies with her own life and he felt sad. There was nothing like a mama and Kristin had lost hers. He looked at her and was glad to see that she and Jessica were laughing at the mismatched little family. The mama turkey would stop and the little guineas would stop also. The second the mama turkey started off again, the little guineas would follow. The turkey gobbled loudly during one of their stops and one little guinea jumped back.

"I think that one just got in trouble," Ora said and Stephen joined the girls in their laughter.

"How did the car get down in the pasture?" Kristin asked.

"The goat's car?" Ora asked as if there might be another car sitting around that he didn't know about.

Kristin nodded.

"Well, the car tore up down there and my brothers were gonna fix it, but they never got around to it."

"But why was it in the pasture?" Kristin asked, as if that concerned her more than the fact that the car had been sitting there forty or fifty years.

"Well, it wasn't the pasture back then, it was the hayfield," Ora answered, as if that should make perfect sense. "That was back when we still lived in the big house up on the hill. I built this house for Mama and me later on. The transmission went out on the truck just a little while after the car tore up. And then the tractor tore up the next spring."

"I think it's really funny when the goats get on the tractor," Kristin smiled, looking at a little black goat that was sitting in the seat of a rusted tractor a few yards away from the car.

"He thinks he's helping, I reckon," Ora said sincerely. "Thinks he's plowing. That was my tractor. It went out on me right where it's sitting. My brothers were gonna fix that, too, but they never did. You see,

they got kinda busy a—courting." He smiled with fond memories. "That's why nothing got fixed."

"Courting?" Kristin asked.

"Dating, as you would call it. When they had a date, they did their chores so fast, you could hardly keep sight of them. Then they'd take off for the creek to get all cleaned up. Us younger ones would hide out down close to the creek behind some trees and when they'd get out of the water, all clean, we'd throw dirt on 'em and they'd get pretty mad." He laughed heartily at the memory. "They'd holler at us, we'd run, and then they'd have to get back in and wash all over again. No joke."

They were all laughing so hard they didn't even hear Kristin's dad's car until it was way down the driveway. Her dad waved at Ora and Kristin started toward the car.

Jessica ran down to the rabbit pens to check on her favorite baby rabbit and Stephen and Ora were alone. Sometimes Stephen liked it that way. "Kristin's dad is messing up my plans making her move," Stephen confided to him.

"What plans?" Ora asked.

"I was going to marry her."

Ora's head jerked downward and his blue eyes widened as if he had been hit by a lightning bolt. "I'm ten times your age and I haven't even been married yet. I haven't had time to think about it and here you are—God—are you gonna be in the same school as her?"

"No. We'll be in the same middle school, but that's three years away."

"Listen, you just sit tight for those three years—OK?"

"OK," he said, disheartened.

"What about your dad? He move?"

"Yeah, so I can't play for the Braves either."

"You sit tight on that, too. Do the best you can, learn what you can and play hard. Your dad won't get you where you want to go, you'll get yourself there. And don't ever make baseball your God."

Five

"GOING TO ORA'S?" JESSICA ASKED as she saw Stephen coming down the road.

"Yep—wanta go?"

"Sure," she said. She tied Sydney, the koala bear, to her belt and joined him. "I really miss Kristin—how about you?"

He nodded sincerely.

Two boys, James and Robbie, ten and twelve years old, had moved into Kristin's old house. They were fun to play baseball with and shoot baskets, but he still missed Kristin.

"James and Robbie are here," Jessica said, pointing, as they walked down the driveway. The two boys went to the farm a lot. They were distantly related to Ora and Stephen thought that was their extreme good fortune. They knew all of Ora's stories because they had known him all their life.

Jessica and Stephen joined Ora and the boys underneath a shady tree and Jessica blushed when Robbie said *hi* to her. Stephen couldn't figure the whole thing out.

"Tell them about when you had to jump in the tree to get away from the bull," Robbie said.

Ora, motioning with his hands and leaning forward in his chair, as usual, began to tell another story of the meanest bull in the world. "I was walking right down yonder under those big oaks and I felt something behind me. You know how you just feel that sometimes?"

They all nodded.

"Well, I turned around and that bull was standing there, looking at me real mean and lowering his head and swinging his tail back and forth real slow like. That's how you know they're gonna come after you. Sure enough, here he comes. I took off running fast as my legs would carry me, his hoofs sounding like thunder behind me and I could hear him snorting, he was so close. I dared to look back as I ran and I saw him bending down to jab my rear end with those horns. I knew I couldn't outrun him and I knew that my only hope was to get in a tree, but as you can see, the lowest limb is twenty feet. But, I had no choice. I jumped."

Stephen was speechless as he looked at the high branches of the tree, then back at Ora.

"I missed the limb," Ora said seriously.

Stephen wasn't surprised.

"What happened?" Jessica asked.

"Well, I caught it on my way back down," Ora said seriously.

Stephen rolled with laughter and Jessica giggled. Ora had tricked them again. His tone was always so serious, it was easy to be caught off guard.

"Well, Stephen here wants to be a professional baseball player when he grows up—how about the rest of you?" Ora asked with a smile, changing the subject.

"I want to be a professional fisherman and have my own TV show," Robbie said, his fishing pole close by his side, as usual. Robbie loved to fish in the creek, but for some reason, Jessica always hated it when he left. She followed him to the creek one day, but she saw a crawdad and ran home screaming.

"Is that so?" Ora asked of Robbie's plans, leaning forward in his chair with interest.

"I want to be a guitar player," James said.

"What kind of music?" Jessica asked.

"Heavy metal."

"I've done a lot of heavy metal," Ora said in his always sincere tone. "That slider saw over there in the tree, that was heavy metal," he nodded adamantly.

The three boys knew Ora was kidding and Jessica followed their cue and laughed.

"Well, since the *ladies first* rule didn't work here, now you go ahead and tell us what you want to be, Jessica."

"I'd like to work in the theater and on Broadway."

Jessica talked about the theater a lot to Stephen and she didn't mean *Star Wars* or *Rambo or Indiana Jones*, which is what he liked to go to the theater to see. She liked Broadway plays with real live people on stage, not filmed stuff. She always showed Stephen the program and he thought it looked really boring, but he didn't tell her that.

The other boys looked about as thrilled as Stephen, but Ora propped his head on his hand with interest. "My mama was in the theater," he said.

"Really?" she asked, interested.

"She traveled all over the place with a group in the very early nineteen hundreds. I have pictures inside, I'd love to show you. Let me get them."

He returned with pictures and memorabilia of his mama and her acting troupe as well as cold cans of citrus beverage for everyone. Ora's mama was really pretty and obviously adored by many. She had saved postcards that had been sent to her from all over the United States from her admirers. Many had scribbled notes on the back, some of them marriage proposals.

"That's Aunt Effie?" James asked, amazed.

"Yes, it is," Ora said proudly. "It'nt that something? Her troupe did a lot of Shakespeare. Mama could recite anything from Shakespeare. She'd recite with such feeling while she cooked dinner, no joke," he laughed fondly. "I can recite a lot of it, too, but not like Mama could."

"Aunt Effie?" James asked again.

"Oh, yeah," Ora nodded. "My daddy happened to be in the audience one night when they came

through here, performing, and he fell in love with her. He even joined the troupe to be near her, but it didn't last long. He was a farmer at heart, you see. So, he asked her to marry him and she came here and lived a life as a farmer's wife," he said, leaning forward in his chair again.

Jessica was totally engrossed in the memorabilia, but Ora's last words caused her to look up. "She left the theater to become a farmer's wife?" she asked and Stephen cringed a little at her tone. "Why would she give up the theater for farming?"

"She fell in love with my dad, you see," Ora said simply.

"Yeah, dummy," Robbie said and Jessica blushed again. Why did she keep blushing? Stephen wondered.

"Well, I don't know what I'm gonna be when I grow up. I haven't decided yet," Ora said, settling back into his chair, taking a sip from his green can. His tone was never condescending, it was as if he truly were one of them.

They knew they had to get home and Jessica reluctantly parted with the pictures. Puddin' and Cinnamon, Ora's dogs, walked toward the gate with them and Ora followed to close the gate for the night

"How'd the dogs get so dirty?" James asked.

"You'd have to ask the dogs, I don't know," Ora said in a sincere voice. "If there was such a thing as a washing machine for dogs, I'd throw them in, but they don't make 'em," Ora said simply.

—⚏—

"Was Effie beautiful when you knew her?" Jessica asked Robbie as they reached their street.

"We didn't know her. She died before we were born," Robbie answered.

"Mama said she let chickens live in the house," James added.

Jessica gasped.

"I'd say she took to farming real well," Stephen said seriously.

—⟋⟍—

Stephen talked to his mom that night about Ora's mama. He told her about the theater and Ora's mama leaving the troupe to marry. "Do you think she ever regretted doing that?" he asked, thinking of Jessica's words.

"No," his mom said with certainty.

"But she had to do laundry in a wash hole in the creek for six boys and her husband," Stephen said, his eyes wide. Jessica might have a point. Her acting life looked a lot easier. "And she had to work in a garden and —"

"I'm sure she never regretted it, not even for a minute."

"But how do you know?"

Stephen's mom looked him right in the eyes and smiled. "There's nothing dearer to a mother's heart than to have a son who loves her the way Ora loves his mama. The way he smiles when he talks about her is so special. Fame and wealth are nothing compared to that."

"I wonder if the other brothers loved her as much as Ora."

"I'm sure the other brothers loved her a lot, and I think her husband adored her, which is always nice," she said with a wistful little smile. "She was very loved. Did you know that Ora built the house he lives in for his mama? Their original house was further up the hill."

Stephen nodded. "He told me that. Ora never finished the house. He said he will later," Stephen said and his mom smiled.

Six

STEPHEN DIDN'T HAVE TO WAIT three years to see Kristin again. He saw her a lot. He and his mom ran into Kristin and Nathan and their dad at the movies and at the grocery store and at the mall and he began to realize that she really wasn't that far away. Her dad even let her come home with them one time to spend the night and she went with him to Ora's. She had really missed the farm and as she played in the pen with the billy goats, Stephen realized just why he was going to marry her.

The billy goats were trying to eat her shirt and a rabbit was nibbling at one of her socks and she was giggling because it tickled. Most girls would have been screaming for help. Even Jessica, who was still sometimes a great tomboy, didn't like getting in the pen with the goats. She was afraid the goats would butt into her the way they did each other.

Stephen heard a noise behind him and he turned just in time to see Jessica spin out on her bike. She came off the bike on both feet, smiling at her success. Stephen smiled at her performance. The dirt she had stirred up trailed off in the small breeze as she joined Stephen at the gate to the goat pen.

"Come on in here and see the goats. They're in a good mood today," Ora smiled.

Jessica looked petrified. "I don't want to."

"Well, that's OK. It sure is. You don't have to if you don't want to, you sure don't."

Ora's voice was so kind, it was no wonder he could soothe animals as well as people.

"Even the little one is butting heads," Jessica said with a frown, looking at the little goat.

"Look, Ora," Stephen said. "It's only a few days old and it knows how to butt heads!"

"They're born knowing how to do that—not so unlike people," Ora answered simply.

"I butt heads with my step dad all the time," Jessica said sourly.

"Why?" Kristin asked.

"He won't let me walk to the store. My real dad used to let me."

"The intersection is a lot busier than it used to be. It could just be that he worries about you," Ora said kindly.

"He won't even let me walk to Stephanie's house."

"Neither will my mama since they widened the road. I'm glad Ora lives on the same side we do," Stephen said.

"Jessica—your real dad still lived here when they widened the road. He wouldn't let you walk to Stephanie's after they widened it," Kristin said.

Jessica fell silent and Ora looked at her with a knowing smile. "Now your step dad can't help it that he wasn't *born* your daddy," Ora said simply. "And I think you might be holding that against him."

"Born my daddy?" Jessica asked.

"You know what I mean," Ora said kindly, feeding the goats. "If someone was treating any of you wrong, I'd be the first one to speak up, but I think your step dad is a good man. You need to give him a chance."

The rabbit that had been chewing on Kristin's sock had decided to leave his chewing and dig intently in the dirt. "What's the rabbit digging for?" Jessica asked, ready to change the subject.

"Worms," Ora answered seriously.

"I didn't know rabbits ate worms!" she gasped and Ora laughed louder than Stephen.

"They don't, they don't. I shouldn't tease like that, I was just a kiddin'," Ora laughed. "Rabbits just like to dig. It's the way they are."

They walked down toward the cow pasture and Ora sat down in a chair just outside the fence, knowing the three of them would gladly feed the cows. He told them he would be selling some of the cows soon.

"Isn't it hard to say goodbye?" Kristin asked.

"Sometimes." He told them about a cow his brother had raised when they were young. It was a big job, raising a cow all by yourself. His brother had to get up even earlier than usual and work even harder when he got home from school. The brother grew attached to the cow and when the time to sell the cow came, the brother didn't want to sell it. He didn't want the cow to go to the butcher. His daddy told him that it was a hard lesson of farming, but that the cow had to go.

The brother received all the money for the cow, but he didn't spend it for a long time. He was still sad. One day, he saw a boat for sale and he wanted the boat so badly, he spent the money. He took the boat to the muddy waters of the Chattahoochee and he spent every free moment he had learning to navigate. He was generous with the boat and he taught each of his brothers how to navigate as well.

Selling the cow was their first hands on lesson in farming and they all came to understand exactly what they did for a living. They provided food for other people and they were paid for their services. They enjoyed feeding the cow and watching it grow, but they understood that they eventually had to part with it. Otherwise, they would have pastures full of cows and no money and the grocery stores would be short on beef. With their pay, they were allowed to enjoy life. That's what farming was all about.

"Did you like steering the boat?" Stephen asked.

"Only in good weather," Ora laughed. "My brothers were the same, 'cept the one who owned the boat. Now, he was something. He could steer that boat in a storm same as on calm water—no joke. When a storm came over the horizon, we turned the boat back over to him. Anyone can steer a boat in calm water, you see, but it takes someone special to steer a boat in a storm."

—◊—

Kristin thought of her mother a lot that night. She guessed it was because she could see their old house through the window of the bedroom where she was sleeping. Stephen was just across the hall and she thought about waking him, but she just buried her head in the pillow and cried.

She tried to change her thoughts to Ora's, to think about the cows or goats or rabbits or anything. She didn't want Stephen's mom to see her cry. Stephen's mom would try to help, but would end up feeling sorry for her and she had had enough pity to last a lifetime.

Even though she tried to think of the animals, she heard Ora's voice. *Anyone can steer a boat in calm water, you see, but it takes someone special to steer a boat in a storm.* For some reason, those words sank into her heart that night and she took them as a challenge to survive without her mother.

—〰—

Stephen and Kristin went back to Ora's early the next morning and Ora smiled when he saw them. "Just like old times," he smiled sincerely. "I hear you're playing basketball, Kristin."

She nodded. "Got a three pointer last game," she smiled and Stephen gave her five.

"How about you, Stephen? How's baseball coming along?" Ora asked.

"I keep striking out. My mama pitches to me a lot and Jessica pitches to me every afternoon, but I've never had so many strikeouts."

"Maybe your mama and Jessica are bad pitchers," Kristin suggested in Stephen's behalf.

"I strike out when Robbie and James pitch to me, too," he shrugged, not denying that his mom and Jessica might be lacking in the pitching department. "I strike out in the games a lot," he said sadly. "It's to the point where I'm afraid to swing."

"Well, every time you *don't* swing, you know it's gonna be a miss," Ora said adamantly. "And you can't just stand there, hoping to be walked. Granted sometimes that would work, but that's no way to play the game. You might as well sit on the bench."

—m—

Ora's words taken to heart, by spring of the next year, Stephen's batting average was better than ever.

He made the Little League All Star Team and Jessica told Ora before Stephen got there. Ora took her hand and they danced in the pasture.

"Did you hear that?" Ora asked the cows. "Stephen made the All Star Team!" The dogs yapped excitedly at his feet and he leaned down. "It'nt that something?" he asked the dogs. Jessica thought he would have given them five if he could have.

Stephen came walking down the driveway and Ora almost ran to the pasture fence. "Mr. Micky Mantle!" he called loudly and Stephen began to laugh.

—〰—

"I can't believe you're finishing up fourth grade," Ora said a few weeks later. "Time flies. Just another year and you'll be back in the same school as Kristin."

Stephen nodded. He and his mom had run into Kristin and her dad at the mall a few weeks earlier and Stephen had asked if Kristin could go to the movies with them. Her dad said that was where they were going anyway, so they all went together. The next week they did the same thing and Kristin's dad started calling the house a lot and just the night before, Kristin and Stephen had stayed with the same babysitter while her dad and his mom went out alone.

"What in the world are you thinking about?" Ora asked Stephen.

"Kristin's dad is messing up my plans again," Stephen said.

"What's he doing *now*?"

"Dating my mama," Stephen said flatly.

Ora let out a laugh and slapped his knee happily, then quickly subdued himself as Stephen looked at him as if he were a traitor. Ora was glad to see Jessica coming down the dirt driveway.

Jessica had gone from cute to beautiful in the past year and was a better tomboy than ever. She climbed over the fence into the goat pen, not even bothering to go through the gate. She laughed now when billy goats butted against her leg. She patted some of the goats on the head, then climbed back over the fence.

"Looks like the ducks are happy today," she smiled as the ducks splashed in the plastic swimming pools Ora kept filled with water for them.

"Yeah, not much rain lately. They like the pools."

Ora was like a father, good to his children. Buying plastic swimming pools for ducks made Jessica smile. She sat down in an old green metal chair beside Stephen and looked beyond the plastic pools to the old greenhouse. It was absolutely piled full of things, as full as one could imagine and the roof was caved in on one side.

"What happened to the greenhouse?" she asked Ora as Stephen still pouted.

"Well, years ago, I grew a lot of plants in there," Ora said, gladly beginning a story. "One day I figured up how much I spent on the plants and the heaters and everything, you know. It came to about three hundred dollars. Then I figured up how much I sold. It came up to about a hundred and eighty dollars. I guess I'm stupid, I just kept trying and trying and losing about the same amount of money every year. Well, one day, I was chopping down the pecan tree," he said, pointing at a stump, "and I wasn't sure which way I should let the tree fall. I thought maybe over toward the house or back toward the turkeys, and well, before I could decide, you see, the Lord decided," he said, pointing at the smashed side of the greenhouse. "The tree fell forward—right on the greenhouse. Saved me a lot of money in the long run. Sometimes the Lord just decides things," he said, looking at Stephen.

Stephen pouted more.

"So, then, I stored some things in the greenhouse, since I couldn't use it anymore—"

"Several tons," Jessica said quietly and Stephen smiled in spite of himself.

"One of these days, I'm gonna clean the greenhouse out, get down to the foundation and rebuild it—it'll be my work shed."

Jessica and Stephen's eyes were both wide as they stared at the greenhouse and its tons of contents, thinking of what a job that would be and wondering if Ora could manage such a thing.

"My to do list is about four miles long now," Ora laughed as he relaxed in his chair and they breathed a little easier.

"Look at the goats," Jessica laughed. "There's grass inside the fence, but they strain their necks trying to reach the grass outside the fence. That's really dumb."

"It is dumb. But, as they say, the grass is always greener on the other side. Goats are a lot like people," Ora said.

"What kind of flower is that?" Jessica asked, pointing at a leafy plant with dark pink blooms.

"That's a four o'clock. I have some seedlings for your mothers. Don't forget to take them with you when you go."

"Why are they called four o'clocks?" Jessica asked and Stephen wondered just how many questions she was going to ask before the day was out.

"Because they bloom at four o'clock. Every day," Ora smiled contently. "You can set your watch by 'em." Ora looked out across the farm with a smile. "My mama always said this place is a little bit of Heaven and you know, I think she's right."

Jessica smiled. So many people would not be content with the farm, they would want a big fancy house and a fancy car.

"I agree," Jessica said. "It is a little bit of Heaven." She walked to a rabbit cage, opened it, and pulled out a baby rabbit. She stood, holding it, and looking down the hill at the creek that Ora had bathed in when he was a child.

"What's the name of that creek?" she asked.

"Coleman Creek, so long as it's on my property," Ora smiled.

She laughed. Coleman was Ora's last name. A lot of the kids called him Farmer Coleman and he liked that, but he also made it clear that it was OK to call him Ora. Kristin, Jessica and Stephen liked to call him Ora because it was a rarity to get to call an adult by their first name.

Ora looked away from the questioning Jessica, back to the still pouting Stephen. "Sometimes the Lord just decides," he said again.

Seven

THE LORD DECIDED THAT KRISTIN'S dad and Stephen's mom should get married and Ora wasn't the only one thrilled about the union. There must have been a hundred people at the wedding who were just as happy. Ora congratulated them, then joined Stephen at a corner table where he was trying to sort out just how he felt.

"Things don't always turn out like you expect," Ora told him kindly. "As a matter of fact, they rarely do. Why, by the time you're old enough to marry or even date, you might very well realize that Kristin isn't even your type."

"But I also don't like having to move across town—away from you—to their house and I think—well, I think my mama raising two other kids is like that turkey raising the guineas," he said adamantly.

"Well, that all turned out OK with the turkey and the guineas," Ora said thoughtfully. "The guineas get a little nervous around Thanksgiving, though—it's just one of those things that couldn't be helped." Ora's wiry little shoulders began to move with laughter at his joke and as much as Stephen tried to fight it, he laughed, too, at the absurd thought of paranoid guineas at Thanksgiving.

—ɷ—

It only took two months of living with Kristin to make Stephen decide that he did not want to marry her. They fought over everything, they eavesdropped on each other's conversations, they told on each other. Stephen got his mom to drop him off at Ora's and he ran down in the pasture where he saw Ora working on the fence. "You were right, Ora. I do not want to marry Kristin," he said before he even said hello.

"Just don't tell me I'm wise beyond my years because that would be really, really wise," Ora laughed.

It was cold and Ora asked Stephen to come inside. They sat down on chairs by the fire and Stephen laughed as the two dogs jumped onto the two empty chairs, complete with cushions, just for them.

"So how's married life besides the Kristin thing?" Ora asked and Stephen laughed.

"I'm not married."

"You know what I mean," Ora smiled.

"It's OK. Nathan pitches to me a lot. Maybe the Lord decided good, after all."

"He generally does, I've found," Ora said sincerely. "And your mama's happy?"

Stephen nodded. There was no denying that.

"And that's important," Ora said emphatically and Stephen agreed.

"I sometimes have a hard time sharing her," Stephen said honestly.

"Well, of course you do. She was all yours for a long time."

Ora's tone was the same as when he soothed the little animals or assured Jessica it was OK if she was afraid to go in the goat pen. He would never tell Stephen he was being selfish, not in a million years.

"But you know the thing I've found about mamas?" Ora asked conspiratorially, leaning forward in his chair.

"What?" Stephen asked with interest, the fire warm on his face.

"Mamas have so much love in their hearts, no one ever gets short changed. My mama had six boys and she had love enough for every one of them and then some left over. If she would have had thirteen kids, she would have had enough love for every one of them and still would've had some left over. So—just imagine how much your mama has with just three kids to use it on. Don't you worry a minute."

Just as Ora's soothing tone got Jessica into the goat pen without ever pushing, Stephen's mind was at ease. Ora got up to stoke the fire and Stephen noticed how loose his pants were. "Did you lose weight?" Stephen asked.

"Yeah, I got kinda sick first cold spell this winter and I had to go to the doctor. First time I've been to the doctor in thirty or forty years, I can't remember which."

Stephen felt fear run through his body at the thought of anything happening to Ora. "But shouldn't you go for checkups even if you aren't sick?"

Ora nodded and humbly said that he would go again in twenty years whether he needed it or not.

Stephen's mom knocked on the door and joined them, one of the dogs politely giving up his chair for her. Stephen decided that his mom must miss Ora, too, because she stayed a long time.

She asked Ora about the loss of weight and he assured her he was on every vitamin known to mankind and that he would be fine. She suspected that the minute he felt better, he would quit taking the medicine he was supposed to be taking, but she knew there was nothing anyone could do about that.

She asked him how things were going on the farm and he told her he had sold a lot of the cows, but said he had so many calves the population would be back in no time.

"Farming is not what it used to be," he laughed. "Used to be I made money selling a cow. If I were to add up what I spent feeding them and what I made selling them, it might be like the greenhouse project," he smiled, looking at Stephen. "No, not really. I had the privilege of getting to know the cows and feeding them."

Stephen still thought that getting to know the cows and feeding them would make it hard to part with them, but he knew that was the way of farming. Ora had taught him that.

"Besides," Ora was saying, "money doesn't matter. I count my successes in friends and I have you guys."

"We're very lucky to have you, Ora," his mom said sincerely.

—⚊⚊—

Stephen hated not living close to Ora and so did Kristin. It was the one thing they agreed on. He and Kristin visited Ora as much as they could, but their family was a busy one and they didn't get to go to Ora's nearly enough. They longed for the days when they could walk or ride their bikes there.

Ora missed them just as much. He walked to the end of his driveway everyday to pick up the newspaper and he always turned to the local sports. A picture of Kristin's Little League basketball team was in the paper one day and the article said that Kristin was the team's most valuable player. Ora smiled all the way back down the driveway. Another day he read that Stephen had made the All Star Team once again and he strutted like a rooster all the way back to the house.

Ora was covering his gardenias with blankets as Stephen came around the side of the house. Ora was so glad to see him, he got a lump in his throat. "Mr. Joe DiMaggio," he said reverently.

Stephen laughed, a high pitched laugh that told his voice was changing before he ever said a word. Ora

hugged him as if he were his own son, amazed at how tall he was getting.

"How do you like middle school?" Ora asked. He wasn't just asking, he genuinely wanted to know.

Stephen told him that it was fine, that it was fun to be in class with Jessica again and that the school might have their very own baseball team the next year.

"But what about Little League?" Ora asked, concerned.

"I'll play both."

Ora shook his head with a laugh.

"Let me help you with the blanket," Stephen said and Ora marveled that Stephen was tall enough to get the blanket over the gardenias.

"Can you smell the gardenias?" Ora asked.

"Yes," Stephen nodded.

"My mama said that gardenias are what Heaven smells like and I believe she's right."

Stephen breathed deeply and nodded. It was a smell good enough for Heaven, he believed. "Jessica said you won a prize for them last year."

He nodded. "The blooms were incredible. 'Cause I put blankets on them," he shrugged, as if anyone could do it.

But Stephen wondered if just anyone could do it, even with blankets. Ora had the same warm touch with plants that he had with animals and people. He could grow things outside that weren't supposed to live outside. When the Lord decided that the greenhouse had to go, Ora missed some of the plants, so he planted them outside. They lived when they shouldn't have.

"Now how did she know you were here?" Ora asked as Jessica came down the driveway.

"Maybe she came to see you," Stephen said in his high pitched, squeaky changing voice.

"Maybe, maybe not," Ora said, smiling.

"Uh—she—uh—likes Robbie," Stephen stuttered, having figured that out finally.

"Not any more," Ora said wisely. "Not for some time now."

—m—

Kristin came with her dad to get Stephen, and Ora was so glad to see her he couldn't quit smiling. "I've been waiting a long time for you to come and feed the cows," he said happily and she laughed as he hugged her.

She remembered when she was little and really thought that Ora waited for her to come feed the cows. She walked toward the pasture, so much taller and more grown up now, but she pulled the top off the huge container of food and filled her hands as always. She felt the same contentment she had always felt when at Ora's as the cows saw her and began to walk up the hill quickly, as cow walking goes.

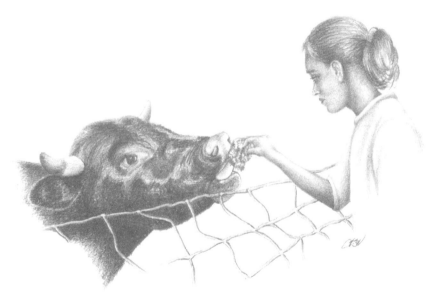

Eight

STEPHEN AND KRISTIN WERE IN high school before they knew it and they still couldn't see eye to eye. They each began to date and Kristin asked Stephen why he dated snobby preps. He told her that he thought it was better than dating dorks as she chose to do. With that question answered, they went on their way.

Ora always read the highlights of the high school baseball games and he knew they were having their best season ever because of Stephen. Stephen played varsity baseball from the moment he entered high school. He had been the driving force behind his middle school successfully starting up their own team and competing well with teams that were already established, so he rightfully played varsity baseball in ninth grade.

—⁂—

Stephen looked at the ice on the blankets covering the gardenias as he walked around the side of the house. He knew that there was plastic underneath the blankets, as cold as it was. Stephen had braces on his teeth and he was so tall Ora barely recognized him when he opened the door.

He was taller than Ora, but Ora reached up to hug him just as hard as he always had, wondering where the little boy with the cowlick had gone. "Get in here right now and get yourself warm, Mr. Henry Aaron."

Stephen laughed, a deep laugh now, and Ora motioned for him to sit down. One of Ora's new dogs gave up his chair for Stephen and Stephen patted the little dog on the head. Puddin' and Cinnamon were older now and didn't offer to give up their chairs, but wagged their tails and panted, looking as if they were smiling, happy to see their old friend. Stephen was glad to see them, too, and he reached over to rub their heads.

"Tenth grade, " Ora said. "Where did the time go?"

"I don't know," Stephen smiled.

"How's Kristin?" Ora asked.

"Toughest bunny on the farm," Stephen answered and Ora laughed, slapping his knee. "Nathan and I walk the line. Sometimes Nathan doesn't even want to come home from college on the weekends."

Ora laughed more. "Is she still playing basketball?"

"Captain of the high school team."

Ora smiled at the news. "Get her to come over here with you sometime."

"I will," Stephen promised.

"I've decided that when it warms up, I'm gonna get to work on the greenhouse," Ora declared. "Since I threw away all that good for nothing medicine the doctor gave me and told me I had to take forever, I'm feeling much better."

Stephen looked a little worried. It was obvious that Ora had never gained back the weight he lost when he was sick, but his spunk was definitely there. "Why the hurry?" Stephen asked.

Ora shrugged, then smiled as he saw Jessica coming in the front door. "I swear, I don't know how she knows when you're here. Radar, I reckon," he said quietly.

"Is he talking about that *'to do'* list again?" Jessica asked and Stephen nodded, hoping she hadn't heard the part about radar.

"It's five miles long now," Ora laughed as Jessica sat down on the sofa.

Stephen looked around the room. There were cards from children hanging on his walls, thanking him for letting them come as a group from many different schools and day cares to visit his farm. Ora had never removed a one, some dating back ten years. Stephen saw his own drawing, made for Ora years back, a picture of Bo Jackson in his Kansas City Chief uniform, number sixteen, slugging a baseball.

Newspaper articles lay on an antique table, some yellowed like the one of him in his All Star uniform and Kristin in her first basketball outfit. Others were new, one a write-up about Jessica playing the lead in the latest high school play.

"Could I ask you two to do something for me?" Ora was asking.

"Of course," Jessica answered without hesitation.

"I know it's cold out there, but I think the animals would like some company. I haven't been able to spend much time with them."

Stephen and Jessica were out the door in a second. Stephen flipped off the electricity to the fence and they headed down the big hill past the bathtubs and toward the old rusted truck and car and tractor where the billy goats played.

Another farmhouse, out of place as much as Ora's in the rapidly developing city, sat quietly in the distance, smoke rolling from the chimney. As they drew closer to it, they could smell the aroma of burning wood.

"I love that smell," Jessica said.

"You? Miss City Girl? Miss Broadway Play?"

"There's nothing like it," she said and Stephen agreed as he watched the smoke blend with the feathery little clouds in the sky.

"Next thing I know, you're gonna give up your theatrical dream and become a farmer's wife," he teased.

"No," she said, shaking her head. "As a matter of fact, this is my last semester. I'm—transferring."

"Where are you going?"

"To New York. There's a high school there that's like—a prep school for the arts. Since I'll be going to college up there anyway—"

"New York?" he asked, knowing that his voice sounded a little more perplexed than he wanted.

She nodded as a little billy goat came up and pressed against her leg. She bent down to pat it on the head.

"What about your parents?" he asked. "Are they going, too?"

"No, they'll be fine here," she said with a smile.

"But—you're in drama club here and you're great in the school plays."

"It's not enough," she said simply.

Stephen could scarcely think straight as they wandered the fields they had played in as children. They walked past cows chewing lazily and Stephen tried to clear his head. When they went back inside Ora's house, Ora took one look at Stephen's face and knew Jessica had told him. Ora knew she would tell him if they were alone and he knew Stephen needed to know so he could have some time to get used to the idea. The animals were a convenient excuse.

"I thought you and your mama were flying to New York this weekend to check things out," he said to Jessica.

"Well, we were, but my mom called for a flight, then I heard her say she just wanted to fly on the plane, not buy it, and that was the end of that trip. We're going in a couple of weeks."

"I always wondered where you got your high spiritedness. Guess it was from your mama, huh?" Ora asked and Jessica nodded.

Nine

ORA WATCHED AS COLLEGES SCOUTED Stephen and he was thrilled when Stephen signed with Georgia Tech. He would be close to home. Kristin went to the University of Georgia up in Athens, where Nathan had gone. Nathan had graduated a couple of years before and was planning to get married in a few months.

Stephen played as hard as he worked at Georgia Tech and time flew past. Ora had to go to the doctor before his twenty year checkup and Stephen came home one weekend in the spring when his mother told him that Ora was sick.

As Stephen came around the side of the house, he was surprised to see the gardenias taller than they had ever been, the blooms more magnificent than ever. A few feet away, he saw Ora, sitting in one of the green metal chairs in the sun.

Ora's head jerked downward like a lightning bolt had hit him when he saw Stephen and he smiled the same old smile, his blue eyes still sharp. "Why, look, it's Mr. Sandy Kofax come to see me, it sure is," he said, standing and walking toward Stephen.

Stephen laughed, his laugh the laughter of a man as he hugged Ora. Ora felt frail beneath Stephen's big hands and he patted him gently.

"Do you even know who Sandy Kofax is?" Ora asked curiously.

"Of course."

"He was before your time."

"That's true, but I know who he is."

"Of course you do. You probably even know his stats."

"I do," Stephen laughed.

"They, Lord—what about that?" Ora laughed.

"My mama told me that you weren't feeling well," Stephen said as Ora sat back down, motioning for Stephen to pull up a chair.

"Oh, she went and told on me, did she? I'm fine now. Doing much better," he said with convincing spunk.

Stephen knew that Ora would say he was doing better whether it were true or not. Ora wasn't one to carry on about himself.

"What happened to the tree?" Stephen asked suddenly as he looked in the direction of the huge oak tree with the swing that he had played on for so many years.

"Lightning," Ora said.

Stephen went to take a closer look. Lightning had hit the tree, leaving a charred jagged mark down the tree's side and splintered wood everywhere, almost as if the tree had exploded.

Stephen didn't need to be working on a college degree to know that the slider saw had probably played a major part in the event. Nothing like a big piece of metal grown into a tree to draw the lightning. He felt sadness as he looked at the pile of wood, metal and swing. No one would ever believe the three things had all been one if they hadn't seen it with their own eyes.

He wanted to call Jessica or Kristin and tell them, but they would probably think he had lost his mind. They were caught up in their own worlds and had probably forgotten just how important all this was.

Of course, he didn't even know Jessica's phone number in New York.

He turned to see Ora looking at him. Ora seemed to be saddened by Stephen's sadness. Trying to recover, Stephen asked if Ora had heard from Jessica.

"Talked to her parents the other day. She's doing well. She's studying hard—she's gonna be a regular Greta Garbo or Betty Grable, that child," he smiled, then asked, "Do you know who Greta Garbo and Betty Grable are?"

Ora wasn't surprised when Stephen answered yes. Stephen wasn't a typical teenager; but then, he hadn't been a typical child. His favorite TV show had always been and still was *The Honeymooners,* a show that was popular twenty-five years before Stephen was born. Stephen wasn't swayed by what was cool at the moment, he liked what he liked. Not so unlike Ora and Ora knew it. They were kindred souls.

Even though Stephen knew quite well who Sandy Kofax was and Greta Garbo and Betty Grable, it depressed him to hear Ora slip into the past so easily. Ora talked about old baseball greats a lot, but he usually threw in quips about the current players and he usually talked about more current movie stars.

Maybe Stephen was overreacting, but it seemed that Ora was slipping away. And there was no way around the fact that the farm was going downhill. Rabbits were hopping around from one end of the farm to the other because their cages were all broken. Some of the doves were out of their cage as well and the gate to the pasture had finally fallen all the way to the ground.

Stephen could no longer view life with the simplicity of a child and say that the cows wouldn't leave because there was no better place to be. He knew very well that one of the cows could wander out of the pasture and get hit by a car and Ora would be held responsible for any damage.

"What in the world are you thinking about?" Ora asked.

"I was wondering what you were gonna do with the tree," Stephen said. That and a million other things.

"I'll chop it up for firewood. It's on my to do list. It'll burn good this winter."

"Let me do it," Stephen said.

"I can do it," Ora said stubbornly.

"I know you can do it, but I want to. That way, when I'm working my rear off at school this winter and can't get home, you'll think about me. Every time you throw a log on the fire."

"I'd think about you, anyway," Ora said, but pointed toward the ax.

The job was more emotional than Stephen had imagined. Making firewood of the tree was like letting go of a part of his childhood, a part of him. He tried to look at it from a farmer's viewpoint. The tree had served its purpose and it would continue to serve a purpose. It would keep Ora and the dogs warm this winter while he was back at school, studying. He could just see the dogs in their cushioned chairs by the fire, watching Ora throw another log on and stoke the fire.

Ora tapped him on the back and he turned. Ora held out the same citrus beverage as always and Stephen felt tears pushing. He opened it, toasted Ora's green can and drank. It tasted like a sip of childhood, but he wasn't a child anymore and Ora wasn't as young as he used to be. Stephen downed the drink and continued chopping wood and fretting.

The last wood splintered away from the slider saw, he took the saw and set it up against the barn, then stacked the firewood. He sadly threw the old swing away, rusted chains and all. He then walked to the doves' pen and began to nail some boards back up.

"That's on my to do list," Ora called.

"I want the doves to remember me this winter, too," Stephen called, still nailing as he wondered just how many more excuses he could come up with.

—m—

Stephen talked to his mom that night about Ora and the farm. His mom was worried about Ora, too, but she assured Stephen that Ora was a tough old soul and kissed him on the forehead before going to bed.

The house quiet, everyone asleep, Stephen picked up the phone and called Kristin. He told her about the tree and the way things were on the farm. She didn't think he was crazy at all, as he had thought she would, she was saddened over the tree and worried over Ora, just as Stephen was. Stephen hung up and fell asleep, exhausted from his afternoon on the farm.

—m—

Kristin lay awake in her dorm room long after they hung up, thinking of her real mother as she did sometimes late at night. She wondered what life would have been like had her mother lived. Not that life was bad, by any means, but still she wondered. She remembered her mother calling her her *baby girl*, she remembered the proud smile on her face. *There's nothing like a mama*, she heard Ora say.

But Ora had also told her many times over that a mama had enough love in her heart for many, many children and he had assured her that Stephen's mama would have plenty of love for her and Nathan and then some left over. And he was right. Stephen's mama had become her new mom, she had become Stephen's sister, he was her brother. They were family. Her new mom seemed to have eyes in the back of her head just like her first mom; she couldn't get away with anything. But most importantly, there had never been a shortage of love—just as Ora had told her there wouldn't be.

She realized just how much Ora had done for them over the years; how much he had helped to make the union of their two separate households smooth, how he had helped in every situation she could remember.

She finally realized that Ora had said the things he said purposefully, and then gone right on with his business as if he hadn't just changed their lives with his words.

She thought of the story of Ora's brother and the boat and almost gasped. Ora had said that his brother was special because he was able to navigate in stormy water, that anyone could steer a boat in calm water. Tears came to her eyes. Ora had known exactly what he was doing all along. He had known she was in stormy water and he was extending to her the challenge to survive without her mother and she had taken that challenge. She wiped the tears and told herself that she needed to go to sleep because she suddenly knew that she would be driving the hundred miles home the next morning to see if there was anything she could do on the farm.

When sleep tried to escape her, Ora and his wisdom once again came to her rescue. *Some people count sheep when they can't sleep*, she heard him say. *Me, I just count my blessings and I drift right off.* She was asleep before she got to ten, Ora the first blessing she counted.

Ten

STEPHEN AWOKE WITH RENEWED vigor and went back to the farm to try and trick Ora into letting him help some more. The gate was open, but there was no sign of Ora outside. Stephen squeezed through the thick gardenia bushes onto the back porch and knocked on the door. There was no answer.

Stephen turned the knob and the door opened. Ora wasn't in the living room and Stephen walked toward the bedroom. He saw Ora in a recliner, perfectly still. Stephen's heart began to pound as he wondered if Ora was OK. He walked closer and saw that Ora was peacefully sleeping. He sighed relief and tried to calm his pounding heart. He could use this time to go fix some things outside. Ora couldn't argue with him if he were asleep.

As Stephen reached the back door, it opened in his face and both he and Kristin let out noisy gasps of surprise, but Ora still slept. "Kristin?" he asked, not believing what he saw.

"Is he OK?" she asked.

Stephen nodded. "He's sleeping. Let's fix the pasture gate before he wakes up," he said, opening the breaker box on the back porch. He flipped the electricity off and they took a look at the fallen gate.

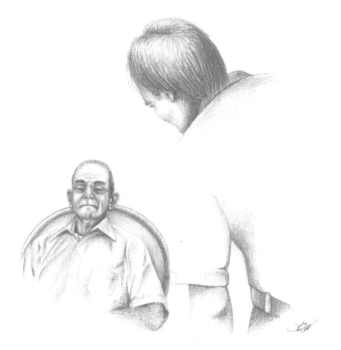

Stephen grabbed a hammer and started working. The pasture was far enough away from the house so that their hammering wouldn't wake Ora. The gate was back up in no time and Kristin started to feed the animals.

"He's low on food," she told Stephen.

"I'll go to the store in a little while," Stephen said. "I'm going to fix some of the pens first."

He found most everything he needed in the greenhouse, all kinds of wood and nails and wire. Kristin joined him and they repaired the rabbit pens and the goat pen and even replaced some wire on the chicken pens before Ora woke up.

He came to the door to see what the noise was and Stephen and Kristin went inside. Ora looked weak and he went back to the recliner, telling them to get a drink if they wanted. They did and he told them they had better be visiting with the animals, nothing else. No repair work. He would get around to it soon enough. They said OK.

He began to drift back off and Stephen looked at Kristin, worried. Kristin wondered if they should get a doctor.

"You know," Ora said groggily, "I wished last night that I had a phone. The first time I ever wished that."

"Did you need a doctor?" Kristin asked quickly.

"No," he said simply. "Jessica came over here the minute Stephen left and I wanted to call him so bad I couldn't see straight," he said. "Her radar was off a little bit, I reckon."

"Jessica!" Stephen gasped, unable to hide his surprise, then he wondered if Ora was talking in his sleep or out of his head. As Ora's head rolled to the side in sound sleep, Stephen sadly decided that he was just living in the past.

"Gardenias," Ora mumbled. "Smell the gardenias."

Stephen's eyes widened. *Heaven*. Ora always said that Heaven smelled like gardenias. "We gotta get a doctor," he said, running out the door.

Kristin followed and they called their mom on Kristin's car phone and asked her who Ora's doctor was. She gave them the doctor's name and number and they called him immediately.

Ora was surprised to be awakened by the old doctor who still willingly made house calls. Kristin and Stephen waited on the porch for what they feared would be bad news.

Stephen heard a car pull down the dirt driveway, but he couldn't see the drive for the gardenias. Some-one got out of the car and he heard the sound of rat-tling paper bags. He walked down the two steps off the porch and around the gardenias and the corner of the house to see who had come to visit. A young girl walked toward him, a huge bag of rabbit chow cover-ing her up to her nose.

"I'll take that," Stephen said politely to the uniden-tified girl and she willingly handed it to him. He dropped it as he realized who she was.

"You sure you don't want me to carry it?" she asked with a laugh, her blue eyes laughing, her face the face of an angel. "I think I was doing a better job of it."

"Jessica!" he gasped.

"Hi, Stephen," she smiled, reaching out to hug him, the rabbit chow at their feet.

"You were really here last night?" Stephen asked, suddenly feeling a little sheepish for doubting Ora.

"Yeah," she said. "Ora said you had just left. I noticed that the animals were kinda low on food, so I bought some. The car's full."

"We'll help you unload," Kristin smiled and Jessica gave her a hug as they walked back toward the car. Girl talk chatter began between the two of them and the doctor emerged from the house followed by Ora, looking stronger than ever. Ora stood on the porch, hands on his hips and watched the unloading of the car.

"What'd you give him?" Stephen asked.

The doctor shook his head. "Nothing."

"I want all three of you in here," Ora said as the doctor went toward his car.

They all went inside.

"When I am too old to run this farm, you'll be the first to know. As for right now, I'm not too old and I won't have you running home from New York and Athens or Atlanta even, worrying about me. I'm a little behind, I admit it. I've been under the weather. You'd get a little behind, too. You'd have to do make up work at school just like I have to play catch up here. Why the tarnation did you call my doctor?" he asked.

"I thought you were dying," Stephen said honestly. "You were talking about Jessica being here—"

"She is here," he said flatly, pointing at her.

"I know that now. You were really tired and you were talking about smelling gardenias and you always said that Heaven smelled like gardenias—"

"Don't you smell them? The windows are up all over the house and you can smell them—"

Stephen cringed as his nose registered the light scent of gardenias.

"I've heard of being scared senseless, but not scared sniffless," Ora said as he headed toward the door. "So—what were you doing out in the yard all morning?" he asked, walking out into the yard.

"We fixed the pasture gate because I was afraid a cow would get out and get hit by a car and you would be responsible," Stephen admitted. He had no choice but to admit it as Ora stared at the gate.

"I realize that it is not ideal that the gate fell, however, the fence is electric. You know that. More importantly, the cows know that. They touch it once and they stay clear of it. The gate still had electricity flowing. The wire didn't break, as you know. That's why you turned the electricity off to work on it, I assume. The gate would have shocked the cows had they stepped on it. So to think that a cow would come to that small opening and gracefully jump over the fallen gate is a little presumptuous, although I'm sure the cows appreciate your vote of confidence."

Stephen cringed and Jessica fought laughter.

"As for the food being a little low, I admit I missed a trip to the store last week. I go on Mondays," he said, placing his hand on the side of his trusty little gray Chevy pickup truck. "I knew I had enough food to make it. I also know exactly how many bunnies I have, how many goats, how many cows and how many chickens. I count them every day and although some may be on the wrong part of the farm, I know they're here. I know what I'm doing."

"I owe you an apology," Stephen said sincerely.

"*We* owe you an apology," Jessica said and Kristin agreed.

"No one owes me an apology, except that confounded wolf that has kept me up three nights straight trying to steal the chickens," Ora said kindly, yawning. "I admit, I was a little under the weather, but if I wouldn't have lost so much sleep, I'd be fine by now. It means the world to me that the three of you care enough to do what you did, but you need to be concentrating on your schoolwork. When I'm old, I'll tell you—OK?"

"OK," they all said.

"OK, so right now, I'll admit I don't feel like going

down there and getting the goats out of the lower pasture because I'm tired. So—if you would do that for me, I'd appreciate it. Since you got their pen fixed and everything, you might as well put them back in it," Ora said, yawning again and heading back toward the house. Kristin followed Ora and Jessica and Stephen went to get the goats.

"I feel like an idiot," Stephen said.

"At least you only drove from Atlanta. I flew from New York when my mom told me he was sick. I'm a bigger idiot."

"You're right. You are," Stephen laughed.

"You don't have to be so agreeable."

"Hey—look—Ora's neighbors are bigger idiots than any of us. They have a fire going."

"I think they win the prize. It's warm out here."

"I think old people get cold easier," Stephen said. "Their circulation or something."

She nodded. "They also haven't been nailing boards all morning and buying the store out of heavy bags of pet food," she laughed.

"I guess we have worked up a little sweat," he said as they stopped and watched the smoke swirl into the sky.

"I'm glad their circulation is bad," Jessica said of the people in the little house at the foot of the hill.

"That's not very nice," Stephen said.

"I mean I'm glad they have a fire. I love the aroma of the wood," she said and he smiled. He had a feeling she was going to say that.

He laughed and sat down under one of the big trees and watched the smoke, loving its aroma as much as Jessica did. Jessica sat down beside him and they watched the smoke drift lazily skyward, engulfing them with its rich aroma.

"It takes me back a hundred years to sit here," she smiled. "From right here, you can just imagine this farm the way it used to be. Rolling land, smoke coming from everybody's chimney because there was no other way to stay warm."

"Corn planted in rows, horses in the pasture," Stephen said.

"Cooking dinner in the fireplace or on an iron stove, washing clothes in the creek. A big family and a big, thriving farm."

"Hardship and happiness," Stephen said and she nodded.

They looked at the pretty blue sky and the wispy clouds. It looked as if the smoke from the chimney had floated to the sky and resided there.

"I thought you guys were getting the goats," Kristin said as she came down the big hill toward them.

"The goats were in no hurry and neither were we," Stephen said.

"Sounds like something Ora would say," Kristin laughed. "Speaking of things Ora says, a lot of them ran through my head last night after you called me," she said, sitting down with them. "That's why I drove here."

Jessica smiled. "That's exactly what happened to me. My mom had been trying to get me to come home for a visit for weeks and I kept thinking I couldn't get away. After she told me Ora was sick, we hung up and Ora's voice just came into my head, all the things he ever said to help me and I called her back and told her I was coming." She seemed to be fighting tears. "Ora taught me a lot about acceptance—my stepfather, mainly. My stepfather is a very good man and always has been. I just didn't want to accept him and Ora knew that all along. Remember when Ora told me that my stepdad couldn't help it that he wasn't *born my daddy*?"

Kristin nodded, laughing at the memory.

"He does have a way with words, doesn't he?" Stephen laughed. "How does Ora know so much? He wasn't from a broken home, yet he had all the answers."

"Absolutely," Kristin agreed. "Remember when Mom and Dad were getting married?" she asked Stephen and he nodded. "I was afraid Mom wouldn't love me much."

"She always loved you—even when you were just the neighbor."

Kristin smiled. "Ora told me that mamas had enough love for a lot of kids and that she would love me a lot."

Stephen smiled. "He told me the same thing."

"You?" Kristin asked. "But you knew that she loved you."

"I was afraid of sharing her. I wasn't being stingy, I was just afraid. I told Ora and he told me the same thing."

"What would we have ever done without him all these years?" Kristin asked.

"Life wouldn't have been the same," Jessica said. "He always said the simplest things that made so much sense."

"Like—*every time you don't swing the bat, it's a miss?*" Stephen asked with a smile.

Jessica laughed. "Boy, did that end up having an impact in your life."

"Kinda."

"Kinda?" she asked. "You're a little modest. I know the pros are after you already. I know you've been asked to quit school and play pro."

"How do you know so much?" he asked.

"I just know," she said and he smiled at her. Something stirred in her heart with the smile and she dropped her eyes from his.

"A hundred years ago, huh?" he asked looking out over the farm, changing the subject

"Yes," Jessica nodded. "A simpler time."

"People always say that, but was it really? What do you think, Kristin?" Stephen asked.

"I think it's simpler to use the bathroom in the house than go to an outside toilet, so I think these are simpler times."

"My sister, the romantic," Stephen laughed and they rounded the goats up and headed toward the goat pen.

The moment the goats were in the pen, they stuck their heads through the wooden rails and began to eat the grass on the outside, causing Jessica to lapse into laughter. The grass was plentiful in the pen, especially since the goats had been gone for a while. It looked better than the grass outside the pen, but still the goats wanted the grass on the other side of the fence.

"Just like people, as Ora would say," Kristin smiled.

"Ora is the only man I know who is happy with what he has," Jessica said seriously. "He doesn't think the grass is greener on the other side. He just calls his land a little bit of Heaven and is happier than a millionaire."

"It's a good way to be," Stephen said and the girls agreed.

Eleven

STEPHEN WENT BACK TO GEORGIA TECH, still feeling a little sheepish that he had underestimated Ora. Kristin laughed all the way back to Athens. The joke was on them, no way around it. Jessica flew back to New York, thinking of Stephen and the smell of the wood burning and the conversation they had shared as they sat under the tree together.

Ora watched Stephen's college career and smiled as the professionals continued to scout him. He knew Stephen would sign with the Braves when he graduated and he did. It was on TV one night.

Jessica saw it from her college dorm and tears of joy ran down her face. She remembered the little boy with the cowlick who was always afraid he wouldn't play for the Braves because his dad didn't live with him anymore. "You did it, Stephen, you did it," she whispered.

Kristin and her friends at the University screamed louder than they had screamed at any of their pre-graduation parties and that was pretty loud. Stephen's mom went by Ora's and they danced around the dogs in the living room.

—⚉—

Stephen was the rookie sensation of the year. He hit the ball so hard, Ora swore it echoed in his pastures all the way from downtown Atlanta. Stephen was always the fourth batter, the cleanup man in the lineup. Anyone who had managed to get themselves on base knew they would be coming home when Stephen got up to bat.

When the Braves were out of town, the crack of Stephen's bat seemed to vibrate in Ora's heart and he always threw his arms in the air about the same time Stephen did as the ball sailed over the fence.

—⚉—

"Mr. Babe Ruth!" Ora said as Stephen got out of his red sports car. "I'm glad you stuck it out in college and got your degree, so if anything were to fall through, you could still pay for that car."

Stephen laughed and hugged the kindly old man. "Don't worry," he said. "It's paid for."

"They, Lord—what about that?" Ora asked. "I heard you got yourself an apartment in Atlanta, too."

"Yeah. I needed to be closer to the stadium," Stephen nodded. "Heard from Jessica?" the inevitable question came.

"Her parents say she's working on her masters," Ora said proudly. "She'll be in New York a while longer. They say she might live there. I don't understand why the two of you don't exchange phone numbers—don't make a lick of sense to me."

"Like you said, she's probably gonna live in New York, I'm gonna live here," Stephen shrugged.

"Things change," Ora said. "Besides, you'll probably be up there playing ball, you could go see her or something."

"There's not a lot of time for visiting on road trips," Stephen said.

Ora sighed and shook his head. The two of them were obviously meant for each other, but they sure were messing it up.

—〰—

Jessica came home two weeks later and Stephen had just left for Yankee Stadium. Ora stomped his foot in frustration. "You two need to communicate," he told her.

"He's busy," she said, shaking her head. "He's flying all over the place and playing ball. He doesn't have time for anything else right now."

—ɯ—

Kristin married Robbie that fall. She had run into him after college and they were engaged in no time. Nathan and his wife added twin girls to their family just after Kristin's wedding. Nathan's first child, a little boy called Austin, had just turned four and was already a frequent visitor to the farm.

"Look at the tom turkey, showing off his feathers," Ora told the little boy in a conspiratorial whisper.

"Is he showing off for me?" Austin asked.

"No, he don't much care what we think, he's showing off for the hens."

Stephen laughed and remembered being a child. Ora was having trouble with his truck and Stephen was tuning it up for him. Stephen wanted to buy him a new truck, but Ora would hear of no such thing.

"I have Jessica's phone number and you are to dial it," Ora told Stephen. "I hate to meddle, but the two of you aren't doing worth a flip on your own, so I have no choice." He handed him a crinkled piece of paper.

Stephen laughed and took the number.

—ɯ—

Stephen called her and she told him she had seen the Braves and Dodger's game on TV. She watched *every* game on TV, but she didn't tell him that. She told him she had heard that Robbie and Kristin got married and asked him to send her congratulations.

"That's very noble of you," he teased and she laughed. "What happened to you and Robbie anyway?" Stephen asked.

"There never was a *Robbie and me.* He never stopped fishing long enough to know I existed and you know it. It was a childhood crush on my part only. Did he become a professional fisherman as he had planned?"

"No, his brother did. James has a TV show."

"That must have ticked Robbie off."

"Probably. It would have ticked me off if Kristin had played for the Braves."

She laughed. "So what is Robbie doing?"

"He's a school teacher at our old elementary school. So is Kristin."

"I never would have imagined that scenario," she laughed.

"Me, either."

Stephen had a plane to catch and he told Jessica goodbye. They made no promise to talk again, although they both wanted to. Jessica felt lonely as the connection was broken and Stephen felt lonely on the plane.

—∭—

Ora couldn't have been more proud if Stephen were his own son. He watched the game that night, the Pittsburgh Pirates beating up on the Braves. Ora strutted like a rooster as Stephen hit the ball, the crack of the bat resounding across the stadium. The Pirates were tough, their pitching precise and the ball didn't clear the fence. Stephen was lucky to make it to second, the two runners before him making it home, tying the score. The next batter popped a fly ball and the inning was over.

The Pirates seemed to be in a foul mood that night, playing rougher and tougher than the Braves. The Pirates were ahead again in no time. In the bottom of the eighth inning, Stephen was trying desperately to tie the score once again. He was on third and he tried

to steal home. "Never gonna make it," Ora said aloud to the dogs.

Ora was wrong. Stephen was safe, but his knee wasn't. The score was tied, but Stephen was writhing in pain on home plate. Ora wasn't sure what exactly had happened other than Stephen slid, the ball came in and the catcher toppled down on top of Stephen, driving Stephen's knee into the ground. Stephen was taken off the field on a stretcher and Ora could care less if the Braves won or lost.

Ora paced the floor until the eleven o'clock news came on, then he sat down heavily on a chair. It was the top story and the sportscaster started with the good news that Stephen's run had won the ballgame. Ora waved his hand at the sportscaster in annoyance. The bad news was that Stephen's career may be over. His kneecap was separated, ligaments were torn and Stephen was being flown home for surgery.

Jessica was crying when her mom called to see if she had heard and she told her mom she was coming home.

Twelve

Mr. Bo Jackson—how bad's the damage?" Ora asked as Stephen came around the side of the house a month later on crutches.

"Well, they wired my kneecap back together and the ligaments—"

"I know all that, I heard it all on TV, play by play. How's the mental damage?"

"Minimal," Stephen said thoughtfully and Ora looked at him quizzically.

"I know how long you've wanted to play—most of your life," Ora said honestly. "I know what it meant to you. I know how hard you've worked. This has to be tough."

Stephen nodded. "No argument there."

"Then how is it minimal?" Ora asked kindly.

"Well, you see," Stephen said, looking at Ora squarely, "I never made baseball my God."

Tears came to Ora's eyes and he fought them. "You'll always be Mr. Bo Jackson to me," he said, swallowing hard. Stephen smiled as Ora reached up to pat him on the shoulder.

"Have you seen Jessica?" Stephen asked.

He nodded. "Not as much as you have, though. I heard she was right beside you the whole time."

Stephen nodded. "She's not going back to school. We're going up to get her stuff in a week or so."

"We? Is that right?" he asked happily. "What made her decide to come back for good?"

"Well, I asked her to marry me and she thought it was a good idea."

Ora almost knocked Stephen off his crutches hugging him. "You know, if the next life is any better than this one, I don't think I can stand it," he declared seriously.

Stephen laughed and hugged the little man who meant so much to him, then confided in him once again. "I told her I would move to New York and she said no."

"Well, it's a good thing. You would last up there about as long as my daddy lasted in that acting troupe."

"But—she gave up the theater for me, Ora," Stephen said guiltily.

"I know of another story that started that way. It turned out real good," Ora said, nodding adamantly. "Don't you worry."

—⁓—

Jessica and Stephen stood looking over the pasture down on the little cottage where the people with poor circulation lived. Smoke rose from their chimney as always, even though it was late spring. The wedding was in two weeks and all the plans were made.

"You do remember that she's a mite spunky, don't you?" Ora asked Stephen.

"Yes, I do," Stephen answered.

"And you do remember that he's Mr. Bo Jackson— he'll have all your kids playing ball, won't matter whether they're boys or girls."

"I know that," Jessica answered.

"OK—if the two of you can live with those things, I certainly can," Ora said, as seriously as if he had just conducted a real counseling session. "Where is it you're gonna be working?"

"Just a few miles from here," Stephen answered. Stephen had been hired as electrical consultant on a big construction job and Ora was glad. He was even happier that Stephen had finished his education instead of quitting school to play ball the way more than one team had asked him to do.

"You know, you might make as much money being Mr. Electrical Engineer as you made playing for the Braves."

"I doubt it," Stephen laughed, "but it doesn't matter. I count my successes in friends and I have you."

The tears were obvious in Ora's eyes, although he tried to hide them. He loved to hear his words come back to him in this fashion. This wasn't the first time by far; there were three generations of kids repeating his words.

"How's your mama?" Ora asked.

Stephen smiled a special smile at the mention of his mama. "She's fine. It took her a little longer to recover from my injury than it did me, but she's OK now."

"There's nothing like a mama," Ora said once again, shaking his head. "Does she still have that big patch of four o'clocks?"

Stephen nodded. "I set my watch by them," he said.

Ora laughed, slapping his knee. "Where is it you told me you're going on your honeymoon?" he asked Jessica.

"Aruba," Jessica answered.

"I don't know where Aruba is, I don't reckon," Ora said thoughtfully. "Where you gonna live when you get back from that place?"

"In my apartment for a while. Then we'll buy land and build a house," Stephen said. "We have to build a big house because we want kids and Jessica is going to teach drama in the basement. She's going to perform in local groups here and she's going to teach it at home."

"That's great, it sure is," Ora nodded thoughtfully. "Remember when I told you that I'd let you know when I was too old to handle the farm?"

"Quite well," Stephen smiled.

"Well, I'm not saying I'm old exactly, but I'm a little tired and I was wondering if—well, if I gave you the land on the other side of Coleman Creek over there, then that'd be one less thing you'd have to buy. And then I'd have you close by, you see, and you could help me sometimes with the animals after you got home from work."

"You couldn't give us the land—" Stephen started.

"Yes, I could. It's mine to give," Ora said as if he were explaining a fairly simple concept to a child. "And I won't take money for it and I want you to live over there so you can help me, so I'm the one asking you a favor. The least you can do is accept. Talk it over—I have things to do over here."

Jessica looked at Stephen with wide eyes. "The house would overlook Coleman Creek and the little cottage where the people with bad circulation live. We could watch the smoke year round," she said, then her eyes brightened even more. "And we could have our own fireplace and our own smoke."

"A big fireplace in the den," Stephen said.

"Our kids could grow up right here—can you imagine that?" she smiled.

"That would be wonderful," Stephen had to agree as he considered Ora's offer.

"Tell him yes," Jessica said after a few minutes. "Tell him yes."

"OK," Stephen said, nodding agreement, appreciative of Ora's generosity.

"Now I'm not saying I want to walk with bulls or anything," she said quickly.

"And no chickens in the house," Stephen said.

"I'll try to refrain," she smiled.

They glanced at the smoke swirling toward the sky one more time, then walked toward Ora to tell him that they planned to be his neighbors.

Ora was so happy he couldn't quit smiling and once again swore that if the next life were any better than this one, he didn't know how he could stand it.

"You knew all along that Stephen and I we were meant to be together, didn't you?" Jessica asked thoughtfully.

"Well, sometimes the Lord just decides things," Ora said humbly, "but He let me in on this one and did I ever have a hard time convincing the two of you!" he laughed, shaking his head and pretending to wipe sweat.

His laughter lessened to a smile and he looked at the two of them, remembering the little boy with the cowlick and the little girl with the koala bear and tears came to his eyes. He walked to them and put an arm around each one.

"Come on," he said. "Let's go see your new place."

They walked through the pasture toward the creek and crossed at a shallow spot, using the rocks as stepping stones, as they had done for years. When they reached the other side of Coleman Creek, Stephen and Jessica smiled as they stood silently and looked across the land, imagining the house where they would live and raise their children, all in the shadow of Ora's farm.

Epilogue

I HOPE YOU ENJOYED THE STORY—no matter what your age. I wanted you to know about this wonderful man called Ora. And if you are a young reader, I wanted you to know that a lot of kids have things happen in their lives that they really wish wouldn't have—like Kristin losing her mother (true story) or like Stephen's dad not living with him (true story). I also wanted you to know that step parents can really work out well.

I have found the saying *God works in mysterious ways* to be true. What you might think is a hardship many times turns out to be a blessing, something that strengthens you or makes you a better person. Have you ever heard that saying—*God doesn't promise us a rose garden but he does plant a seed within each one of us?* It's true.

ABOUT THE ARTIST

Applauded by national magazines and television as "One of the World's Foremost Pastel Artists", Jim Wonderling has had more than thirty major art shows throughout the world. He has also had numerous television appearances where he was celebrated as the only person in the country to use the painstakingly complex pastel technique which he developed. Jim's artistic focus has been primarily on auto racing, but a chance meeting with the author, Marcia Carter, and her husband Ron, presented Jim with the opportunity to illustrate this book. With their support and the encouragement of his friend, Steve Free, Jim has returned to his artistic roots and his art career.

To Order Books

 CALL   (770) 281-3101
 FAX   (770) 234-6110

INTERNET   http://www.blacksands.com

EMAIL   sales@blacksands.com

MAIL   Black Sands Enterprises
P.O. Box 4382
Canton, GA 30114-0017

ITEM	QUANTITY	COST	TOTAL
Ora's Farm	_____	$16.95	_____
Stephen's Moon	_____	$9.95	_____
Merchandise sub-total			_____
Shipping & Handling*			_____
*$3.50 for 1st book, $1.95 for each additional			
Georgia residents please add 6.00% sales tax			_____
TOTAL			_____

Sold To

Name _____

Address _____

City _____

State / Zip _____

Phone _____

Email _____

Please make checks payable to Black Sands Enterprises.

❑ Visa ❑ MasterCard ❑ American Express ❑ Discover

Credit Card # _____

Expiration Date _____

Name on Card _____

Authorized Signature_____

Please allow 2–4 weeks for delivery
Thank you for your order!